GIFT OF

John Warren Stewig

Carthage

Copyright © 1991 by Nord-Süd Verlag AG, Gossau Zürich, Switzerland
First published in Switzerland under the title *Der weiße Rabe und das schwarze Schaf*
English translation copyright © 1991 by Nord-Süd Verlag AG, Gossau Zürich, Switzerland

Library of Congress Cataloging-in-Publication Data
Sopko, Eugen,
[Weisse Rabe und das schwarze Schaf. English]
The white raven and the black sheep / Eugen Sopko:
translated by Helen Graves.

Translation of: Der weisse Rabe und das schwarze Schaf.
Summary: A white raven and a black sheep, each an outcast because
he is a different color from his fellows, try to gain acceptance by
switching places and discover along with their peers that color is
not everything.
ISBN 1-55858-118-9
[1. Prejudices—Fiction. 2. Self-acceptance—Fiction. 3. Ravens-
-Fiction. 4. Sheep—Fiction.] I. Graves, Helen. II. Title.
PZ7.S715Wh   1991
[E]—dc20   91-7254

British Library Cataloguing in Publication Data
Sopko, Eugen
The white raven and the black sheep.
I. Title II. [Der weisse Rabe und das schwarze Schaf].
English
833.914 [J]

ISBN 1-55858-118-9

1 3 5 7 9 10 8 6 4 2

Printed in Belgium

THE
White Raven
AND THE
Black Sheep

WRITTEN AND ILLUSTRATED BY

Eugen Sopko

TRANSLATED BY

Helen Graves

North-South Books
New York

Up in the sky, far away from the village, a flock of ravens soared over the fields and meadows. They were looking for food.

All the birds were black except one fledgling. This one little raven was as white as a sheep.

Sometimes a group of men came along and shot at the ravens. They usually aimed at the white raven, because he was so easy to see, and he had to fly especially fast to get away from them.

The other birds were angry at the white raven. "It's your fault these men are shooting at us!" they crowed. And they chased the little bird away.

Next to a herd of white sheep, there was a new lamb.
He was just like all the other lambs. He played happily and
was very good at hide-and-seek because he could hide in the
shadows. This little sheep was as black as a raven.

Sometimes a wolf stalked the sheep. Everyone in the herd thought the black sheep was to blame. "Get away from us, so the wolf will leave us alone!" they bleated. And they drove the little sheep away.

The white raven and the black sheep were sad and lonely.

"Why aren't I black, like all the others?" the raven said to himself.

"Why can't I be white like my brothers?" the little sheep murmured sadly.

But just when they could hardly bear the loneliness anymore, they met each other in the forest.

They told each other their sad stories.

"I wish I were white like you," said the sheep.

"If I were black like you I would be so happy," said the raven.

"Let's stick together and see what we can do about this," said the sheep.

Then they curled up next to each other and soon were fast asleep.

"I have an idea!" said the raven in the morning. "At the very edge of the forest I saw some old cans of paint the villagers have thrown away."

"So what?" asked the sheep. "What's that got to do with us?"

"I can paint you white, you can paint me black, and then we can go back to our friends."

"What a good idea!" exclaimed the sheep, and off they went to find the dump.

When they had finished painting, the sheep congratulated the raven on his cleverness.

But suddenly a few drops of water fell from the sky. Soon the rain was pouring down, washing away all the paint. The raven was white again and the sheep was black.

"O dear! What will we do now?" they cried.

"If we can't change our appearance, then we'll just have to trade places," said the raven.

"What do you mean?" asked the sheep curiously.

"You're black, you can go to the black ravens. And I'm white, so I'll go to the white sheep."

"Yes, that makes sense," agreed the sheep.

And so the sheep went to find the ravens. They all played together for a little while, but finally the ravens told him, "You may be black like us, but you can't fly. Our white raven looks strange, we admit, but he does know how to soar up into the sky. We want him to come back!"

The white raven flew over the fields and meadows until
he found the sheep. They played with him for a time, but
then the ram said, "We know you're white like us, but you
have a hard beak. Our black sheep does look strange, but
he's very soft. We want our little black sheep to come
back!"

Once again, the white raven and the black sheep met in the forest.

"The ravens miss you, and they want you back if you're willing to return," said the sheep.

"And the sheep want you to come home, too, because you belong to them," said the raven.

So the black sheep went back to his herd and the white raven returned to his flock. But they remained friends forever.